NEW MEXICO

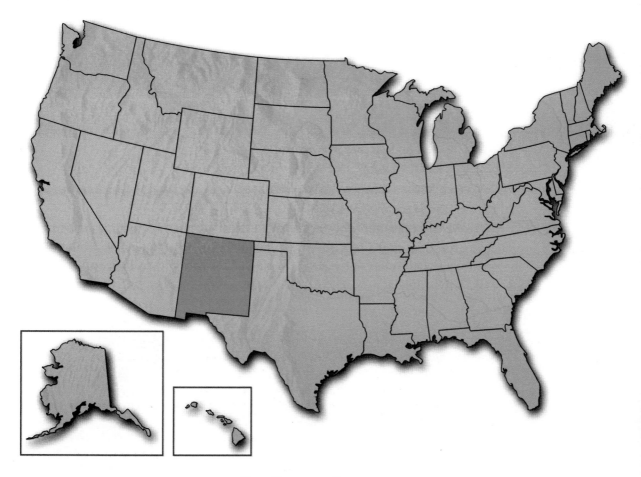

Rennay Craats

Published by Weigl Publishers Inc.
123 South Broad Street, Box 227
Mankato, MN   56002
USA
Web site: http://www.weigl.com

Library of Congress Cataloging-in-Publication Data available upon request from the publisher. Fax: (507) 388-2746 for the attention of the Publishing Records Department.

ISBN 1-930954-74-3

Printed in the United States of America
1 2 3 4 5 6 7 8 9 10   05 04 03 02 01

Editor
Jennifer Nault
Copy Editor
Diana Marshall
Designers
Warren Clark
Terry Paulhus
Photo Researcher
Diana Marshall

Photograph Credits
Every reasonable effort has been made to trace ownership and to obtain permission to reprint copyright material. The publishers would be pleased to have any errors or omissions brought to their attention so that they may be corrected in subsequent printings.

Cover: Adobe Architecture (Corel Corporation), Flowering Cactus (Corel Corporation); **Kindra Clineff:** pages 4T, 20B; **Corbis Corporation:** pages 15T, 26T; **Corel Corporation:** pages 3B, 6T, 7B, 10B, 11TL, 11B, 12T, 13T, 15B, 22B, 23T, 23BL, 24B, 25B, 29BR; **Courtesy Museum of New Mexico, #13682:** page 19T; **Courtesy Museum of New Mexico, #20206:** page 17B; **Courtesy Museum of New Mexico, #71390:** page 17T; **Courtesy Museum of New Mexico, #9843:** page 19B; **Edward S. Curtis, Courtesy Museum of New Mexico, #117080:** page 18B; **Wyatt Davis, Courtesy Museum of New Mexico, #132058:** page 16BL; **Digital Stock Corporation:** page 5BL, 29BL; **Anna Koopmans:** pages 8B, 14T, 18T; **Steve Mulligan Photography:** pages 8T, 10T, 12BR; **New Mexico Department of Tourism:** pages 3T, 3M, 6B, 7T, 7ML, 12BL, 13B, 14BL, 21B, 28B; **PhotoDisc, Inc.:** pages 5T, 14BR, 27B; **Photofest:** pages 24T, 25T; **PhotoSpin, Inc.:** page 28T; **Sarbo:** pages 4B, 9T, 9B, 11TR, 20T, 21T, 22T, 23BR, 26B, 27T; **Marilyn "Angel" Wynn:** pages 16T, 16BR.

CONTENTS

INTRODUCTION

Southwestern cuisine reflects a blend of Native-American and Hispanic American cultures. Common ingredients include tortillas, pinto beans, and chilis.

QUICK FACTS

New Mexico is 121,598 square miles in size. It is the fifth-largest state in the country.

The state got its name, *Nuevo Mexico*, from Spanish explorers in the 1560s. They hoped to discover riches similar to those of the Mexican Aztecs'. The name was changed to New Mexico when the area became a territory of the United States in 1850.

The capital of New Mexico is Santa Fe. The largest city in the state is Albuquerque.

Its scenic beauty is the primary reason visitors travel to New Mexico. From snowcapped mountains to scorching deserts, New Mexico, nicknamed the "Land of Enchantment," has it all. In terms of culture, the state is a fascinating blend of Native-American, Hispanic, and European traditions. Descendants of the Native-American Pueblo peoples have lived in the state's southwest longer than any other culture in the United States. New Mexico is an interesting mix of ancient and modern influences. The state is home to portions of the first road, *El Camino Real*, built by Europeans in the United States. This road dates back to the sixteenth century.

By contrast, some of the most sophisticated research facilities in the world are found in New Mexico. The first atomic bomb was built in the state in 1945, and scientists in New Mexico continue to experiment with nuclear power and space exploration into the twenty-first century.

Santa Fe, whose name means "Holy Faith" in Spanish, is one of the oldest towns in the United States. It was founded 13 years before the pilgrims landed at Plymouth Rock.

Getting There

New Mexico is a nearly square state in the country's southwestern region. It is bordered by Colorado to the north, and by Oklahoma and Texas to the east. Texas is also to the south of New Mexico, and Arizona provides the western border. New Mexico shares a border with the country of Mexico as well. The Mexican states of Chihuahua and Sonora lie along the southwestern part of New Mexico. Along with Arizona, Utah, and Colorado, New Mexico is one of the Four Corner States. The corners of all four states meet at the same point.

Traveling by automobile in New Mexico is made simple with about 60,000 miles of highways. Drivers heading east or west often use Interstate 40, and those driving north or south can take Interstate 25. There are 171 airports in the state, many of which are privately owned. The main airport in the state is Albuquerque International Sunport. About 3.3 million people pass through the Sunport every year.

QUICK FACTS

Since 1925, New Mexico's official colors have been red and yellow. These are the colors of Spain.

New Mexico's state motto is "It Grows as it Goes."

In the early 1900s, the railroads were an important means of transportation in the state. While most of the old railway lines are no longer in use, several freight and passenger lines remain.

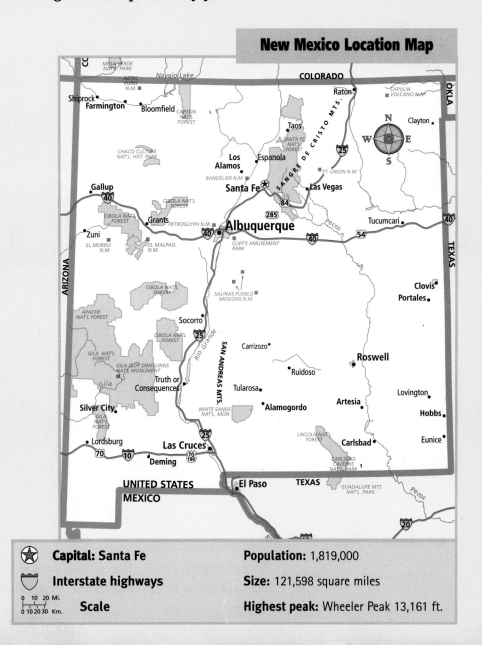

New Mexico Location Map

⭐ **Capital:** Santa Fe		**Population:** 1,819,000
🛡 **Interstate highways**		**Size:** 121,598 square miles
Scale 0 10 20 Mi. / 0 10 20 30 Km.		**Highest peak:** Wheeler Peak 13,161 ft.

The Native Peoples in New Mexico carved large holes in the cliffs, linking them to form clusters of dwellings.

In the 1870s, New Mexico was as wild as any other region in the West. The residents of the state's towns included an unruly mixture of miners, cowboys, gamblers, and cattle **rustlers**. Most carried guns, and were quick to use them. Some towns did not even have sheriffs or deputies to keep the peace.

Out of this lawless frontier arose one of the most well-known outlaws in the history of the United States—Billy the Kid. Born in New York City in 1859, William H. Bonney moved to New Mexico with his mother in 1873. He soon became involved in a bitter **rivalry** between cattle merchants, known as the Lincoln County War. While still a teenager, Bonney claimed to have killed twenty-one men, including the Lincoln County sheriff and two deputies, earning him the nickname "Billy the Kid." In 1881, Sheriff Pat Garrett shot and killed Billy the Kid at Fort Sumner. At the time of his death, Billy the Kid was only 21 years old.

QUICK FACTS

In the 1870s, a newspaper summed up the violence of the West. It reported: "Everything is quiet in Cimarron. Nobody has been killed in 3 days."

When Billy the Kid was 13 years old, he moved to Silver City with his mother. He was arrested, and escaped from prison for the first time, when he was 15 years of age.

New Mexico's official state song is "O, Fair New Mexico." It was written in 1917 by Elizabeth Garrett. She was Sheriff Pat Garrett's daughter.

Kit Carson and Buffalo Bill Cody are also famous cowboys from New Mexico.

Still behind bars after all these years, people can visit Billy the Kid's gravesite, which is protected from vandals and souvenir seekers.

The Rio Grande, the nation's second-longest river, is rich in frontier history.

The Rio Grande is the longest river in New Mexico. It crosses the entire length of the state, flowing from north to south. Water from the river is used to irrigate crops along the river valley. While it may be long, the Rio Grande is actually quite shallow, preventing it from being used as a shipping route. **Tributaries** of the Rio Grande include the Rio Puerco and Red River. Water is scarce in New Mexico—the state has less than 240 square miles of this precious natural resource. With the exception of West Virginia, New Mexico has the least amount of water in the country. Water bodies, such as lakes and rivers, take up only 0.002 percent of the state's land area. Many riverbeds have run dry, leaving some regions of the state dusty and arid. Most of New Mexico's lakes are human-made reservoirs. The largest lake in New Mexico is the Elephant Butte Reservoir, which was created by damming the Rio Grande.

QUICK FACTS

The state flag is yellow, and a red sun with rays appears in the center. This symbol is called a "Zia." It is an ancient Native-American symbol that represents four things: the four directions, the four seasons, the day (sunrise, noon, evening, and night), and life (childhood, youth, middle age, and old age.)

In 1950, a black bear cub was trapped in a tree during a forest fire in the Lincoln National Forest. The forest was destroyed, but the cub, named Smokey, survived. Smokey became the mascot for National Fire Safety. In 1963, the black bear was selected as the official state animal.

In Mexico, the Rio Grande is called the *Rio Bravo. Rio* is Spanish for "river."

Ancient Native-American ruins, such as the Tyuonyi Ruin, are examples of some of New Mexico's earliest settlements.

The land in the canyon of the Jemez Mountains is extremely fertile.

LAND AND CLIMATE

New Mexico is made up of four land regions: the Great Plains, the Rocky Mountains, the Basin and Range Region, and the Colorado Plateau. The Great Plains, **dissected** by canyons and rivers, cover the eastern third of the state. The Rocky Mountains cover the north-central region toward Santa Fe. Here, the Rio Grande winds through towering mountain ranges. The Basin and Range Region, an area with mountains and deep valleys, is southwest of the Rocky Mountains. The Colorado Plateau is found in the state's northwest. It features plains, valleys, cliffs, and **mesas**. Badlands with dry lava plains are a feature of the southern part of the Colorado Plateau.

New Mexico's climate is exceptionally sunny and dry throughout the year. The average temperature is about 60° Fahrenheit in the south and about 50°F in the north. During summer, temperatures as high as 100°F are common. The average annual precipitation in the state is quite low—13 inches. Nearly half the rainfall occurs in July and August.

New Mexico's dry landscape is dotted with black lava formations that date back 800 years.

QUICK FACTS

Santa Fe is 7,000 feet above sea level. This makes it the country's highest capital city. About 85 percent of the state has an elevation of over 4,000 feet.

The highest point in New Mexico is Wheeler Peak. It is 13,161 feet high.

Albuquerque, New Mexico, ranks third in the nation for the average days of sunshine it receives per year.

Average Daily Percent of Possible Sunshine

Phoenix, AZ	81
El Paso, TX	80
Albuquerque, NM	76
Miami, FL	68
Portland, OR	39
Juneau, AK	23

Lake Valley was once the site of a booming silver mine. Today, it is an abandoned ghost town.

NATURAL RESOURCES

New Mexico is among the leading mineral producers in the country. Oil is a very important natural resource to the state. Eddy, Lea, McKinley, San Juan, and Chaves Counties all have major oil fields. During the 1990s, New Mexico ranked seventh in the country for petroleum production and fourth in the production of natural gas.

Copper is New Mexico's most valuable non-fuel mineral. One of the largest copper mines in the world is the open-pit Chino mine near Santa Rita. It is also the oldest active mine in the region. The Chino mine is about 1 mile long and 2 miles across. This pit produces about 136,000 tons of copper each year.

Silver is mined in the state. In Lake Valley, miners found silver that was so pure, it did not need to be dug out of the ground using traditional methods. Instead, it could be sawed off in blocks. In 1882, one silver nugget was valued at $7,000, which amounts to about $120,500 today. The silver strike was one of the largest in U.S. history. By 1900, silver was devalued and Lake Valley's silver mining declined. The state continues to produce silver as a **by-product** of copper **smelting**.

Natural gas and oil account for approximately 80 percent of New Mexico's total mining income.

QUICK FACTS

In the United States, only Arizona and Utah produce more copper than New Mexico.

New Mexico's major natural resources are oil, natural gas, uranium, potash, copper, coal, zinc, gold, and silver.

New Mexico is the country's leading producer of perlite, the second-largest producer of pumice, and the second-largest producer of mica.

Coal is a valuable natural resource in the area. The York Canyon Mine supplies a great deal of coal to states in the upper Midwest.

New Mexico was once home to the "Uranium Capital of the World." The state supplied most of the United States's uranium after World War II and during the Cold War period. By the 1990s, however, uranium production slowed because of a decrease in demand.

PLANTS AND ANIMALS

About 25 percent of New Mexico is covered with trees. The state has five national forests, including the Gila National Forest, which is the largest in the country. It covers 3.3 million acres.

New Mexico's official flower, the yucca, grows in the state's dry areas. This plant, which looks like a pincushion with white flowers, is known by many names. New Mexicans called it "soapweed" because early New Mexicans used the roots to create hair tonic and soap. They also used the pointed tips of the yucca leaves as needles for sewing. These sharp, long leaves earned it another nickname, "Spanish bayonet." Yucca leaves can be woven into rope, baskets, and even sandals.

Many of the desert's cacti are threatened species. The Sabo Preserve, in San Juan County, is working to protect the Knowlton cactus. The location of the preserve is kept secret because it is the only place in the world where the Knowlton cactus is found.

The yucca was selected by schoolchildren as the state flower on March 14, 1972.

QUICK FACTS

In May 2000, a controlled fire was set to clear away dry bush. This was done to prevent forest fires. Instead, the wind fanned the fire, and it was soon out of control.

The other national forests in New Mexico are the Carson, Cibola, Santa Fe, and Lincoln national forests.

Many wild plants, such as the creosote bush, the desert marigold, the desert zinnia, and the sunset cactus, grow in New Mexico.

There are fourteen threatened or **endangered** plants in New Mexico, including the Sacramento Mountains thistle, the Sacramento prickly-poppy, and the gypsum wild-buckwheat.

The hedgehog cactus is well-suited to the dry climate of New Mexico.

The roadrunner, New Mexico's official bird, can run up to 15 miles per hour. This state symbol was adopted in 1949. At the time, the roadrunner was known as the Chaparral Bird. The roadrunner is also known by its Spanish name, *El Correcaminos.*

The Gila Riparian Preserve covers 7,308 acres in Grant County. It protects threatened and endangered animals. The Gila woodpecker and the southwestern willow flycatcher live in the preserve.

The Mexican long-nosed bat, the Mexican spotted owl, the whooping crane, the Gila trout, and the least tern are all endangered animals that are found in New Mexico.

The Carlsbad Caverns are home to tens of thousands of bats. One chamber in the cavern is more than ten football fields in length.

The Rio Grande Zoological Park in Albuquerque displays more than 1,300 animals in exhibits much like their natural habitats, including a rain forest and an African **savanna**.

Elk, deer, sheep, and porcupines live in forested parts of the state. The desert areas are home to jackrabbits, coyotes, and javelinas, which are animals that resemble large boars.

Due to their large size, some species of tarantula are capable of preying on frogs and lizards.

The endangered Mexican wolf population has dwindled to about 200 in the world. Conservationists are re-establishing a Mexican wolf population in the United States. They introduced thirty-four wolves into the national parks system in 1998 and 1999, and these animals now roam freely through Arizona's Apache National Forest and New Mexico's Gila National Forest.

A smaller and more abundant New Mexican creature is the tarantula hawk wasp, New Mexico's official insect. While this metallic-blue wasp with red wings enjoys feasting on the nectar of milkweed flowers, it also eats much larger prey. The wasps often fly into a tarantula's nest for a meal. Despite the tarantula's size and poisonous fangs, the hawk wasp often wins the battle.

Coyotes roaming New Mexico's plains are able to move at speeds of 25 to 30 miles per hour, which makes them powerful predators.

Galleries along Canyon Road draw many tourists to Santa Fe.

TOURISM

Tourism is important to the economy of New Mexico. Every year, more than 12 million people travel to the state to experience the recreational, historical, and geographical wonders that New Mexico has to offer. Santa Fe is the top destination city for visitors throughout the year. It is located in the beautiful Sangre de Cristo Mountains, and is known for its Spanish and Native-American art. More than 100 art galleries can be found along Canyon Road, the main street of Santa Fe. Santa Fe draws history buffs, as well. The city boasts the oldest house in the nation, which has been standing since the early 1700s, and the oldest continuously occupied church, which was built in the 1620s.

The supernatural also draws tourists to New Mexico. Roswell is home to the International UFO Museum and Research Center. This museum is devoted to **phenomena** related to unidentified flying object (UFO) sightings and landings in the United States. With its investigation of a possible alien spacecraft crash and its **alleged** cover-up, the museum is an international center for UFO information. The New Mexico Tourist Association has named the International UFO Museum and Research Center the top tourist attraction in the state.

Due to strong westerly winds, the sand dunes at the dazzling White Sands National Monument shift about 20 feet per year.

The White Sands Missile Range is known as "The Birthplace of the Race to Space."

INDUSTRY

A nuclear energy research company, Sandia National Laboratories, has operated in Albuquerque since 1945. It employs more than 6,600 people in New Mexico. Over the years, this company has developed and tested rockets and weapons as well as safe methods of transporting nuclear weaponry. In 1997, NASA's Pathfinder probe to Mars touched down successfully, thanks to Sandia National Laboratories. The company designed the Pathfinder's landing air bags.

One of the best examples of the importance of scientific research to New Mexico can be seen just west of Socorro. There, twenty-seven enormous dish **antennas** can be found. These dishes, called the Very Large Array (VLA), make up the largest radio telescope in the world. Each antenna is 81 feet wide and weighs more than 200 tons. The telescope receives radio waves from distant galaxies. Scientists use the readings to learn about the universe.

While many industries in New Mexico are high-technology industries, the state relies on more conventional industries as well. Printing and publishing, electronics, and stone and glass production are thriving industries in the state.

The twenty-seven dishes that make up the VLA are aligned in a Y-shaped configuration.

QUICK FACTS

Rockets are tested at the White Sands Missile Range, which is located on the same land where the first atomic bomb was tested.

Sandia National Laboratories is a world leader in scientific research.

The VLA has an information center for visitors. People can learn how radio telescopes work and how the dishes and antennas are assembled.

The hotel tycoon Conrad Hilton was born in San Antonio, New Mexico. During the 1940s, Hilton bought some of the most luxurious hotels in the United States.

Ranching is an important industry in New Mexico. It accounts for about two-thirds of the state's farm revenues.

New Mexico is a leading state in the production of chili peppers, with more than 21,000 acres under cultivation.

QUICK FACTS

Farmland takes up more than 44 million acres of state land.

The federal government employs about 25 percent of New Mexican workers. The state and local governments are major employers as well.

Corn, cotton, peanuts, apples, and pecans are valuable field crops in New Mexico.

pecan orchard

GOODS AND SERVICES

Despite its arid climate, agriculture is important to the New Mexico economy. Successful irrigation, using water from rivers or **aquifers,** has made farming possible. Every year, ranching and farming contribute more than $2 billion to the state's economy. Unlike other states, the number of farms and ranches in New Mexico is growing. Today, the number stands at more than 15,200. Cattle, including beef cattle and dairy cattle, are the top agricultural product. Eggs and hogs are also key farm products. Hay, chili peppers, and onions are the state's leading crops.

More than 90 percent of the electricity generated in New Mexico comes from steam-driven power plants. These plants burn **fossil fuels**—most often coal—to produce electricity. Most of the state's electricity is produced in the Four Corners area, in the northwest, and is sold to other states. The Four Corners Power Plant is one of the world's largest fossil-fuel steam-driven power plants. It takes about 10 million tons of coal every year to run the five boilers at the plant.

Cattle ranching is the leading agricultural activity in New Mexico. Ranchers raise beef cattle in almost every part of the state.

Intel, the world's largest manufacturer of computer chips, chose New Mexico for its $1 billion expansion because of the state's well-educated work force.

QUICK FACTS

About 42 percent of New Mexico's work force are employed in the service industry. People working in restaurants, hotels, and museums, as well as those in hospitals, real estate, banks, and law offices are all service workers.

New Mexico's military bases include Cannon Air Force Base in Clovis, Holloman Air Force Base in Alamogordo, and Kirtland Air Force Base near Albuquerque.

The War Eagles Museum in Santa Teresa displays fighter planes from World War II, jet-fighter aircraft from the Korean War, and antique cars.

Until the 1900s, New Mexico had very few public schools. Before 1888, there were no public colleges or high schools in the state.

Manufacturing is important to the state's economy, earning about $3.9 billion each year. Albuquerque is the major industrial and manufacturing center in New Mexico. Electrical equipment tops the list of New Mexico's manufactured goods. Two major electronics companies have large offices in Albuquerque. Honeywell Defense Avionics manufactures military communication systems. Its parent company, Honeywell, employs 125,000 people worldwide in areas such as aerospace, automation and control, and transportation. Intel Corporation also operates in New Mexico, where it manufactures silicon chips for computers. Intel invented the microprocessor, and more than 80 percent of personal computers use these microprocessors.

Space products are also valuable goods in New Mexico. The aerospace industry began in 1930, when a Massachusetts man, Robert Goddard, came to New Mexico to experiment with rockets. Although some people thought his ideas were crazy, his experiments created a valuable industry in the state. Since then, New Mexico has been a leader in missile, weapons, and space-related research and manufacturing. The government funds several top research laboratories, as well as military bases, throughout the state.

The University of New Mexico, based in Albuquerque, is the state's largest university, with more than 30,000 students in attendance.

FIRST NATIONS

The first Native Peoples in New Mexico hunted bison and mammoths. The Mogollon were the first to grow crops. They lived in the region along the New Mexico–Arizona border.

The Anasazi were another prominent group of Native Peoples in the area. They grew corn, beans, squash, and cotton, and tamed wild turkeys. The turkeys provided the Anasazi with meat for food and feathers for clothing. This highly developed civilization built multi-storied apartment houses. Some of these buildings, such as the Pueblo Bonito, had more than 600 rooms. The Anasazi abandoned their homes suddenly. Historians think that a drought that lasted from 1276 to 1299 drove the Anasazi away. They moved toward the Rio Grande Valley, where they lived alongside the Pueblo.

During the fifteenth century, the Navajo and the Apache came to the New Mexico region. The Navajo settled just west of the Pueblo, who taught them how to raise beans and corn. The Apache spread out over eastern and southern New Mexico. These peoples were accomplished hunters and strong warriors. By the mid-1500s, explorers began arriving in New Mexico in search of riches.

The Apache used mostly baskets and animal skins as carrying devices.

QUICK FACTS

More than 25,000 Anasazi sites have been unearthed by **archeologists** in New Mexico.

In 1864, thousands of Navajo started the long and dangerous journey to Bosque Redondo Reservation, known as the Long Walk.

Stone spearheads have been found at Folsom. These artifacts suggest that Native Americans hunted in northeastern New Mexico at least 10,000 years ago. The spearheads are known as Folsom points.

New Mexico's Navajo, the nation's largest Native-American group, share their art and culture by offering demonstrations, such as wool spinning.

EXPLORERS AND MISSIONARIES

The first Europeans to visit New Mexico did so accidentally. Alvar Núñez Cabeza de Vaca and his crew of 300 were stranded on the Texas coast in 1528. Only Cabeza de Vaca, a Moroccan slave named Estevanico, and two others survived diseases and conflicts with Native Americans. For 8 years, Cabeza de Vaca and his group ventured west, across Texas, and then south, to Mexico City. They encountered many Native Peoples who told them about a kingdom of riches called the Seven Cities of Cibola.

Many people began searching for these fabled cities. Estevanico, Cabeza de Vaca, and a priest named Marcos de Niza set off in 1539 for Cibola. They turned back after a conflict with Native Peoples. Father Marcos told the Spanish that the Zuñi Pueblo was larger than Mexico City. In 1540, explorer Francisco Vásquez de Coronado traveled to Zuñi to claim the promised riches. He found nothing but mud huts.

Alvar Núñez Cabeza de Vaca came upon New Mexico when he was stranded after becoming separated from his expedition's ship.

QUICK FACTS

In 1539, Estevanico guided Father Marcos de Niza on an expedition to discover the Seven Cities. Zuñi Pueblo peoples killed Estevanico during this trip.

Pedro de Castaneda, who traveled with the Vásquez de Coronado expedition, wrote about the journey. Castaneda's account was first published in translation in 1896.

Francisco Vásquez de Coronado explored New Mexico and Arizona.

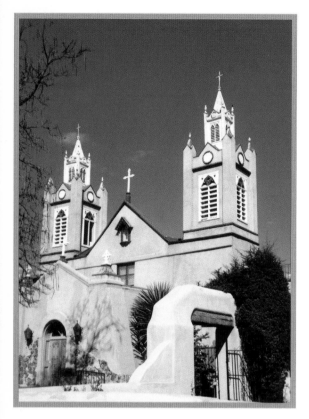

The San Felipe de Neri, in Old Town Albuquerque, is the city's oldest church, having been built in 1706.

In the early 1600s, Spanish Roman Catholic priests established the first schools in New Mexico.

When Oñate returned to Mexico, he faced charges of mistreating the Native Peoples. He was convicted of misconduct while in office, in 1614.

In 1692, the Spanish governor Diego de Vargas reclaimed the area. Colonists and priests returned to New Mexico. They built homes and missions in and around Santa Fe.

EARLY SETTLERS

In 1581, a group of soldiers and missionaries from New Spain entered New Mexico to learn about the Pueblo peoples. Later, in 1598, Juan de Oñate led a group of settlers to New Mexico to try to convert the Native Peoples to Christianity. He became the governor of New Mexico.

Roman Catholic priests from Spain worked in vain to convert the Native Peoples to Christianity. There were many battles between the church, Oñate's civil authorities, and the Native Peoples. The Acomas thought they would be spared because they lived in a village on top of a 357-foot-high mesa. The only way to reach it was via steep, uneven stairs in the rock. Oñate's nephew made it to the top, and a conflict erupted between the Europeans and the Acomas. When Oñate heard that his nephew had been killed, he sought revenge. He ordered that the Acoma village be destroyed, which resulted in the deaths of nearly 800 Native Peoples. After this massacre, Oñate was forced to return to Mexico and was relieved of his duty as the governor of New Mexico.

Today, the ancient 70-acre Acoma Pueblo, known as "Sky City," is the oldest continuously inhabited city in the United States.

Juan de Oñate's colony was the first European settlement in New Mexico. It was established at the Pueblo of San Juan de Los Caballeros, near the Chama River. After Oñate's disgrace, Pedro de Peralta became governor and moved the state's capital to Santa Fe.

In the 1800s, trappers and traders from other parts of the United States arrived in New Mexico. Feeling threatened, Spanish officials chased many of them out of the area or threw them into prison. In 1821, Mexico won independence from Spain and opened the area to American traders. That year, trader William Becknell cleared the Santa Fe Trail to transport goods from Missouri to New Mexico. American colonists continued to push west into New Mexico, causing conflict between America and Mexico. When the Mexican War broke out, the United States took control of the region.

At first, growth in the territory was slow, but soon New Mexico's towns began to grow, and were filled with cowboys, miners, gamblers, cattle rustlers, and railroad workers.

Santa Fe is the end point of the 800-mile Santa Fe Trail.

QUICK FACTS

Albuquerque was founded in 1706. The Spanish farming village was named in honor of a province in Spain.

In 1800, there were 10,000 New Mexicans living along the Rio Grande in the north.

New Mexico became the forty-seventh state on January 6, 1912. At the time of its statehood, New Mexico boasted a population of 330,000.

John Chisum owned 80,000 cattle in eastern New Mexico in the 1870s. He was the country's biggest cattle rancher at the time.

By blazing the Chisum Trail from Paris, Texas to the Pecos Valley in New Mexico, John Chisum helped create New Mexico's early cattle industry.

POPULATION

Albuquerque has experienced rapid growth in recent decades, with an increase in population of more than 50,000 people between 1980 and 1990.

New Mexico has a population of more than 1.8 million, ranking it thirty-sixth in the country. Almost half of New Mexicans live in the three metropolitan areas of Albuquerque, Las Cruces, and Santa Fe. About 40 percent of the population lives in the Albuquerque metropolitan area.

While more than 70 percent of New Mexicans live in cities, there is still a large **rural** population. About 9 percent of the total population is Native American, many of whom live on reservations in the central and northwestern regions of the state. Forty-two percent of the population is Hispanic American, while the national average for Hispanic Americans is 12.5 percent.

About 7 percent of the state's children in the state attend private schools. Upon graduation, students have twenty-seven public and seventeen private post-secondary education facilities from which to choose.

QUICK FACTS

The population of New Mexico in 1950 was only 681,187. It increased by 40 percent by the end of that decade, another 7 percent in the 1960s, and 28 percent in the 1970s.

The most populated city in the state is Albuquerque, with a population of 448,600. Other large cities include Las Cruces, Santa Fe, Farmington, and Alamogordo.

Today, there are 15 people per square mile living in New Mexico. The national average is about 79 people per square mile.

There is a high proportion of Hispanic Americans in New Mexico. One out of three New Mexican families speak Spanish at home.

POLITICS AND GOVERNMENT

New Mexico's Capitol is one of the newest State Capitols in the United States. It was opened in 1966.

The first seat of government in the United States was established in Santa Fe in 1609.

There has been a great deal of debate over whether nuclear weapons should be tested in New Mexico. The government tested the world's first atomic bomb on July 16, 1945 near Alamogordo. The bomb was designed and made in Los Alamos.

In New Mexico, five judges sit on the Supreme Court, and seven judges serve in the Court of Appeals.

The Green Party is popular in parts of New Mexico, especially in Santa Fe and Taos Pueblo. This political party is dedicated to protecting the environment.

The governor and other executive officials, including the lieutenant governor, secretary of state, and treasurer, serve 4-year terms.

New Mexico's constitution has been in place since 1911. Since then, it has been amended more than 100 times. Amendments and bills are proposed by either the Senate or the House of Representatives in the state's legislative branch of government. If the majority of the forty-two senators and seventy House representatives approve a bill, it is passed to the governor to make into law. If the governor **vetoes** the bill, it can still be passed by the legislative branch if enough people support it.

The governor is part of the executive branch of the government. This branch is responsible for making the laws in the state. It also appoints many important state officials. The judicial branch consists of the state's courts. The highest court in New Mexico is the Supreme Court. The judicial branch ensures that laws are followed.

The Palace of Governors was built in 1610. It is one of the oldest public buildings in the nation.

CULTURAL GROUPS

New Mexico's unique culture is a reflection of the state's three main cultural groups: Hispanic Americans, Native Americans, and people of European descent. About 42 percent of the state's population is Hispanic American. In some villages, such as Truchas and Chimayo, there are descendants of **conquistadors** who still use a form of sixteenth-century Spanish. New Mexico is a **bilingual** state. The official languages are English and Spanish. There are many Spanish newspapers and radio programs in the state.

Hispanic Americans celebrate their culture in New Mexico with a variety of festivals and events. The Spanish Market gives Hispanic-American craftspeople a chance to showcase their art. Each September, the Fiesta de Santa Fe celebrates Hispanic-American culture with dances, concerts, and parades.

At Christmas, *Las Posadas* celebrations use tiny candles, called *farolitos*, to honor the Catholic traditions of Hispanic-American culture.

QUICK FACTS

At Christmas time, New Mexican streets are lined with paper bags holding candles propped in sand. People in the north call these lanterns *farolitos* and those in the south call them *luminaries.*

The first Spanish-language newspaper in the state was *El Crepusculo de la Libertad*, which means, "The Dawn of Liberty." It started circulation in 1834 in Santa Fe.

Mexican cuisine is big in Las Cruces—really big. Every October, the city makes the biggest *enchilada* in the world at the Whole Enchilada Fiesta.

Spanish history can be traced back several generations in New Mexico.

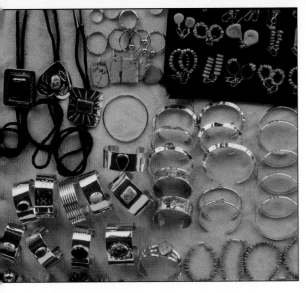

The Pueblo peoples associated turquoise with the sky. Turquoise was traditionally used as a ritual offering or trade item.

Native-American culture is strong in New Mexico. Many of the state's Native Americans live on reservations and celebrate their culture with festivals and ceremonies. Craft traditions, such as the making of turquoise jewelry and woven rugs, have been passed down from generation to generation. Every August, Gallup hosts the Inter-Tribal Indian Ceremonial. This event features powwows, rodeos, arts, and a parade. It also serves as a trade fair for more than twenty Native-American groups in the country.

Some of the festivals and ceremonies that are held during the year allow Native Americans to preserve their traditions. Pueblo feast days are celebrated throughout the state. On Christmas Eve at San Felipe Pueblo, the spirits of animals come to honor the baby Jesus. This mixture of Christianity and Native-American beliefs is fascinating—**rituals** are performed by deer dancers in antler headdresses and buffalo dancers in horned headdresses. San Geronimo Day at Taos Pueblo also features traditional dancing, as well as a trade fair displaying drums, pottery, and clothing. Every year, about 100,000 people gather at the Santa Fe Indian Market, which offers artwork from more than 100 different Native-American groups.

QUICK FACTS

Many Navajo in New Mexico live on a reservation that covers 7,500 square miles of land in the north.

The Native-American reservations are often governed much like separate states.

Cloudcroft Oktoberfest features hay rides and square dances as well as German cuisine.

Each Pueblo village has its own pottery style. For many Native Americans, pottery is an important part of their culture. Some use pottery in birth ceremonies and as part of funeral ceremonies.

Zuñi Olla Maidens carry ornate water pots on their heads during the Gallup Inter-Tribal Indian Ceremonial.

ARTS AND ENTERTAINMENT

In 1929, Georgia O'Keefe spent the first of many summers painting in New Mexico. She finally moved to the state in 1949.

The unique landscape and culture of New Mexico have often served as inspiration for writers and artists. Although born in Oklahoma, author Tony Hillerman lived in New Mexico as a young man. He was fascinated by the Navajo culture and the importance that Native Americans placed on their traditions. His novels, such as *Skinwalkers* and *A Thief of Time*, explore Navajo traditions. Hillerman was one of the nation's most successful mystery writers, with fifteen best-selling novels to his credit. Other successful New Mexican writers include Willa Cather and Pulitzer Prize winner N. Scott Momaday.

New Mexico is also home to many talented artists. Maria Martinez was a well-known potter from the Santa Fe area in the early 1900s. Her black-on-black pottery was delicate and rubbed to a shine. Today, her pots are found in museums around the world. Georgia O'Keefe is another famous New Mexican artist. She took everyday objects, such as flowers, and painted them in an **abstract** way. She spent much of her career painting the New Mexican landscape.

Some of New Mexico's Native Peoples make and sell traditional dolls and handcrafted purses in markets and craft fairs.

Demi Moore has starred in many hit movies including *Ghost*, *The Juror*, and *A Few Good Men*.

QUICK FACTS

Actor Neil Patrick Harris, who was cast in the role of genius child doctor in the television series *Doogie Houser, MD,* is from Albuquerque.

Demi Moore was nominated for a Golden Globe for Best Actress in the 1990 motion picture, *Ghost*.

Slim Summerville, born in Albuquerque, began his acting career during the silent-film era. He appeared in many silent films. In later years, he appeared in *All Quiet on the Western Front,* a popular Hollywood film.

New Mexicans can listen to talented entertainers at many annual music festivals, including the Santa Fe Music Festival, the Clovis Music Festival, and the Chamber Music Festival.

Music and theater lovers have many choices in New Mexico. The Santa Fe Community Theater was founded in 1918, and the Albuquerque Little Theater has been staging performances since the early 1900s. People visit the Santa Fe Opera for the music, as well as the atmosphere. In July and August, the audience at the outdoor theater faces the foothills of the Sangre de Cristo Mountains. The New Mexico Symphony Orchestra in Albuquerque, and several professional and semiprofessional orchestras in other cities, entertain New Mexicans.

Many musicians and actors hail from New Mexico. Roswell's John Denver launched his solo music career in 1968. With smash hits including "Leaving on a Jet Plane" and "Rocky Mountain High," he became a folk-music hero. He won many awards, including a special RCA Award for his album *John Denver's Greatest Hits*. The album sold 10 million copies—an RCA record. Denver continued to entertain audiences until his death in 1997.

Demi Moore was also born in Roswell. She moved from soap operas to the big screen with a debut performance in *Choices* in 1981. In the mid-1980s, roles in *No Small Affair* and *St. Elmo's Fire* brought attention to the actress and led her to Hollywood stardom.

The Albuquerque Folk Festival hosts forty-eight music and dance workshops and three open-jam sessions. Attendees can take in acoustic folk music at this festival.

With a base elevation of 8,600 feet, a peak elevation of 10,677 feet, and a vertical drop of 2,077 feet, Angel Fire is a snowboarder's paradise.

The Unser family, from New Mexico, has dominated auto racing for decades. Brothers Bobby and Al Unser, whose father and two uncles were racers, also pursued the sport. The Unser brothers were successful racers, with Bobby winning the Indianapolis 500 race three times and Al taking the title four times.

Bobby and Al Unser's brother, Jerry, raced in the Indianapolis 500 in 1958. The following year, he died from injuries he sustained in a terrible crash. Regardless of this tragedy, the brothers continued to race.

The Albuquerque International Balloon Fiesta is one of the world's most photographed events.

SPORTS

New Mexico offers many enjoyable recreational opportunities. For instance, Albuquerque hosts the world's largest hot-air balloon festival every October. The Albuquerque International Balloon Fiesta attracts large crowds who watch hundreds of balloons floating above. This event is not a race, but participants do compete. Prizes are given to the balloonist who can best perform certain feats, such as target landing.

Skiing is a favorite sport in New Mexico. Ski areas throughout the state offer fun in the winter as well as the summer. Angel Fire, in the Moreno Valley, is a top ski resort. In winter, snowboarders and skiers are challenged to conquer the slopes or explore the trails on cross-country skis. Angel Fire offers runs for beginner and advanced skiers. In the summer, the trails are open to mountain biking, hiking, and horseback riding. Skiers in this beautiful mountain area are replaced with golfers in the summer.

The Albuquerque International Balloon Fiesta draws more than 800,000 spectators.

While New Mexico does not have teams playing in the major professional leagues, it has been home to some great professional athletes. One of baseball's great players came from New Mexico. Pittsburgh Pirate outfielder Ralph Kiner set offensive records for his team and in the league. During his first seven years as a Pittsburgh Pirate, Kiner led the National League in home runs and was the only person to hit home runs in three straight All-Star games from 1949 through 1951. He also holds the National League record for the most consecutive seasons as the league's top home run hitter, with seven. In his ten years as a Pirate, Kiner twice hit more than fifty home runs in a season, and batted-in 100 or more runs six times. In 1949, he had 127 runs batted-in—a league record. Fans still wonder what Kiner could have accomplished had a back injury not forced him to retire at only 32 years of age. His contribution to the game was officially recognized in 1975, when he was inducted into the Baseball Hall of Fame.

The Rio Grande is home to some of the southwest's best white-water rafting, with rapids for various levels of experience.

QUICK FACTS

Albuquerque's New Mexico Scorpions battle for the Central Hockey League championships. The Scorpions were the division champions in 2000.

The Angel Fire ski area has the state's only freestyle snowboarding **half-pipe** and the only high-speed quad chairlift.

There is great hiking and biking to be had in almost every region of New Mexico, using trails along mesa tops, desert canyons, or high mountain meadows.

Sand surfing is enjoyed on the dunes at White Sands National Monument. People use plastic saucers to ride the "waves."

Baseball is one of the oldest and most popular spectator sports. The game was developed during the early 1800s by children and amateur players.

Brain Teasers

1

What was the lure of the Seven Cities of Cibola?

Answer: The cities were thought to contain incredible riches. The streets and houses were said to be decorated with gold and precious jewels. They also were thought to contain a spring with water that could restore youth.

2

Who was Pancho Villa?

Answer: Pancho Villa was a Mexican revolutionary. After U.S. President Woodrow Wilson supported one of Villa's enemies, Villa and his supporters crossed the border for revenge. They arrived in Columbus where they burned houses, stole guns and other supplies, and killed residents. The U.S. Cavalry arrived ready for battle, but Columbus had already been devastated.

3

What is the "Roswell incident"?

Answer: Roswell has two UFO museums spawned by the "Roswell incident," which occurred in 1947. That year, the government announced that it had found a flying saucer. The government then recanted its claim and said the object was a weather balloon. For decades, people have doubted the second claim.

4

What did Robert Oppenheimer do in New Mexico?

Answer: Robert Oppenheimer helped to create the first atomic bomb. The bomb was first tested on July 16, 1945. It cast a bright orange flash of light that was visible in Santa Fe, 150 miles away.

5

What was the Long Walk?

Answer: In 1864, the U.S. forces destroyed the Navajo's crops, homes, and livestock, to force them to move. The Navajo faced starvation, so had no choice but to relocate. They were forced to walk 300 miles to the Bosque Redondo Reservation in eastern New Mexico. They did not have enough food or proper clothing for the journey, and hundreds died in the snowy mountains.

6

Who were Chiefs Victorio and Geronimo?

Answer: Chiefs Victorio and Geronimo were Apache leaders who led attacks on settlers. Victorio carried on his raids until his death in 1880. Geronimo led the last Apache attacks on settlers until he surrendered in 1886.

7

What is unique about the Tucumcari Historical Research Institute?

Answer: This museum is unlike any other. Its exhibits include displays of barbed wire, bottles, old saddles, and fishing hats. It gives visitors a glimpse of New Mexico's early history.

8

What is *El Camino Real*?

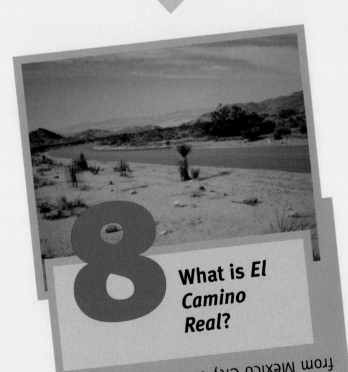

Answer: The *El Camino Real* was the first road established by Europeans in the United States. First traveled in 1581, it ran from Mexico City to Santa Fe.

FOR MORE INFORMATION

Books

Aylesworth, Thomas and Virginia Aylesworth. *Discovering America: The Southwest*. New York: Chelsea House Publishers, 1996.

McDaniel, Melissa. *Celebrate the States: New Mexico*. New York: Benchmark Books, 1999.

Robinson, Maudie. *Children of the Sun; the Pueblos, Navajos, and Apaches of New Mexico*. New York: Messner, 1974.

Web Sites

You can also go online and have a look at the following Web sites:

New Mexico Department of Tourism
www.newmexico.org

Tourism New Mexico
http://usa.dedas.com/states/nm.html

50 States: New Mexico
www.50states.com/newmexico.htm

International UFO Museum and Research Center
www.iufomrc.com

Some Web sites stay current longer than others. To find other New Mexico Web sites, enter search terms such as "Santa Fe," "Albuquerque," "Pueblo," or any other topic you want to research.

GLOSSARY

abstract: creative representation of an idea of an object

alleged: accusation without proof

antennas: conductors by which electromagnetic waves are sent and received

aquifers: formations of rock that soak up moisture to form large reserves of groundwater

archeologists: scientists who study early peoples through their artifacts and remains

bilingual: able to speak two languages

by-product: something produced during the making of something else

conquistadors: Spanish soldiers and adventurers who conquered South America in the sixteenth century

dissected: split up

endangered: at risk

fossil fuels: organic materials, such as oil, coal, or natural gas that can be burned to produce energy

half-pipe: a curved ramp made of snow used to perform snowboarding tricks

mesas: high plateaus with steep sides

phenomena: events that are considered remarkable or extraordinary

rituals: series of actions used in a religious ceremony

rivalry: heated competition

rural: related to the country

rustlers: cattle thieves

savanna: a plain characterized by coarse grasses and scattered tree growth

smelting: obtaining and refining metal

tributaries: rivers or streams that join a larger river

vetoes: using authority to reject something

INDEX

DATE DUE

FEB 0 1 2003		
SEP 1 6 2006		
MAY 1 3 2009		
SEP 0 8 2009		
DEC 0 3 2009		
OCT 0 4 2011		
GAYLORD		PRINTED IN U.S.A.